I0822582

SAFETY IS A RARE THOUGHT

By

Sam Taylor

&

Luis Lopez

Safety Is a Rare Thought

Printed in United States of America

ISBN: 9798218812553

Library of Congress Control Number: 2025921492

Chapter 1 – The Whisper Before the Squall

"Jervis!" I yelled, running through the door.

Sitting down on the living room couch next to him, I started rambling on about my date last night while he stared at the television.

"Man, you should've seen her. Five-foot-nothing with—"

He interrupted me. "Look what's going on. There's an actual serial killer in some ass-neck city in Florida," he said, pointing at the breaking news he'd been watching all morning.

Not really wanting to hear about something that bleak after such an upbeat night, I went to my room. Jervis immediately called me back to the living room. Just as I was walking in, the TV flashed a sketch of the suspected serial killer's face and listed the estimated victim toll at sixteen in just two weeks.

"Wow! Sixteen in two weeks. Someone is seriously pissed about some shit," Jervis said as he shut the TV off.

"Yeah, well, we're in Sioux Falls, so really, who gives a shit, right? I'm about to give this girl a shout and see if she had a nice time last night uptown, and ask if she'd be down to try it again sometime," I replied, already clutching my cell and bringing it to my ear as I left the room.

Heading to the kitchen to make pancakes, I couldn't get the image of that serial killer out of my head. Mixing the batter, I was half-thinking about what was going on in that faraway city and half-listening to Emerson tell some *bird* on the phone he wanted to vibe with her.

"Hey, Emerson, you want some pan—" I started to say when I finally figured it out. Vinny.

I immediately yelled, "Valducci!"

Emerson told the *bird* he was on the phone with that he'd call her back as I was turning the TV back on. There was no mistaking it — the sketch had to be Vinny Valducci.

"So what, Jervis? Valducci on a killing spree? I'm not really surprised. The kid was an *oddball*," I said nonchalantly.

Jervis just stared at me, not saying anything. I knew what he was on.

"Yeah, Vinny was kind of off, but a murderer? Either way, maybe this is the break we needed. Maybe this is our chance to make a name. If we can track him down, talk him down… how sick would that be? Vinny was cool with us in high school, remember?"

I replied, "Yeah, I'm sure he was. So what? We're supposed to go down to—how did you so eloquently put it?—'*Assneck, Florida*,' and be like, 'Valducci, let's go get a beer and talk about this whole killing thing you've been doing'? How far is that place from where we grew up, anyways?"

That's how the conversation between me and Jervis initially went, I think. I was reluctant, but eventually I relented, and we started tracking down past mutual associates in an attempt to piece together Vinny's movements before the killings began.

Finding Valducci proved to be a daunting task; it turned out he had no friends to speak of and never really had a job. This guy was like a *ghost*. How the hell were we going to reach him?

Emerson kept contacting people we knew, but none had seen him in years. Forget friends — this guy didn't have anyone who'd even seen him alive since high school, it seemed. Then, as I was sitting down, flipping through channels trying to find something to get my mind off this madness for a while, I remembered something. Vinny was a huge VHS movie collector. Actually, he wasn't just a collector; he was a *hunter*. He was obsessed with finding mint-condition tapes of obscure '80's horror films — the kind you only find collecting dust in the back of some forgotten rental shop. He called them *survivors*.

I turned to Emerson. "We're headed down south… We're headed home," I said.

Without him saying a word, I knew what Emerson wanted: an explanation.

"Look," I started. "Let's hit that almost-out-of-business video store, *Hollywood Videos*, over in Riverview. Remember Vinny's obsession? I think that'd be a good place for us to start."

"So, *Assneck, Florida*, it is, I suppose," Emerson quipped.

Days went by, and I could think of nothing but getting to Florida. Emerson didn't really seem to be taking this too seriously, but the truth of the matter was we were headed into dangerous territory. I know we had always thought this cat was a non-threat to us, but he did manage to murder sixteen people.

Glancing up at the calendar, I saw we had two days until takeoff. We couldn't sleep, so we stayed up for a while watching a couple of random movies and discussed everything we had planned — in depth this time.

Jervis fell asleep first. Since I didn't like flying, I was just going to stay up and then sleep on the flight. Finally, six a.m.

"Jervis, let's go!" I yelled, turning off the stereo that had been playing *Éblouie par la nuit* on repeat for the last few hours.

"Did you sleep at all, Emerson?" I asked as I wiped the cold from my eyes. No response. Guess he was in the zone.

Chapter 2 – She Was Half a Warning

The world became a blur of highway lights and sterile airport corridors, all of it muffled by our mission roaring in my head. The next thing I knew, I was pressed against a tiny, cold window, the hum of the engines a constant reminder that we were probably flying straight into chaos.

Finally, we touched down in Florida — the old stomping grounds. We both decided not to contact any family. It would be too distracting, and putting family members in potential danger was not something we wanted to do.

Jervis was the first to speak. "All right, we've only got enough time to run in and put our shit away. We've got to get out to that school immediately." He said as we pulled into the hotel parking lot.

The hotel room smelled like bleach and bad decisions. We dropped our bags and were back out the door in under five minutes. The ride to Eisenhower was all highway glare and the hum of tires, the kind of silence that means both of us were thinking the same thing — this wasn't going to be a friendly reunion.

Our investigation started at Eisenhower Junior High. That's where Vinny's pregnant wife Telixa worked as a math teacher. We were able to dummy up some fake press credentials and told the main office we were doing a story on the dangers of teen sex in middle schools. Everyone bought it… well, almost everyone.

"Okay, Emerson, we've got full access," I said as we walked out of the main office.

"Yeah, yeah. Give me that map of the classes, Jervis. We need to find Telixa ASAP," Emerson replied.

Walking down the hall was a real memory-lane deal. Me and Emerson really didn't even need the map.

"You may have fooled everybody else, but I know why you're here," said someone with a loud, obnoxious voice behind us. Of course, it was Telixa. "You already got Chris thrown in jail because of that stripper that OD'd! I can't believe you let him take the fall for that! Now I'm pretty sure the reason y'all came here was for information on Vinny, and it ain't gonna happen!" she continued, crossing her arms and shaking her head.

"Look, I know how you felt about Chris. And he was our boy," Emerson stated.

"He's a grown man, and he made the decision to fall on the sword," Jervis finished.

"Don't worry about this. I got this," Jervis said.

Telixa had always had a secret crush on me, and the years hadn't changed that one bit — not by the way she stared at me. As I started walking up to her, we saw someone standing at the end of the hall on the other side of the building.

"Vinny, is that you?" Jervis yelled, but the figure stood motionless, offering no response initially.

"What the fuck are you doing here? If you knew what was good for you, you would leave as fast as you came," the figure finally said, then ran out the door.

We tried to run after him, leaving Telixa behind, but when we got outside, all we saw was empty space.

"Well, what do we do now?" I asked.

“I think that’s him,” Jervis replied. Following his gaze, I saw Vinny walking toward East Bay High, which was right next to Eisenhower.

“Let’s go!” Jervis yelled.

We ran full speed toward the front entrance and burst through the doors. Vinny was nowhere to be found. The halls were packed with students running around frantically. We searched the whole building, but there was nothing pointing us even remotely close to where Vinny could be.

“What the fuck, seriously, man. Either Vinny knew we were coming—” Jervis started to say.

I cut him off. “Or he was coming to… kill Telixa!”

We darted back over to Eisenhower as fast as we possibly could, but when we got there, Telixa lay in the hallway. Well, half of her did. The other half was nowhere to be found. Teachers and security guards stood frozen — some with hands over their mouths, others turning away, their faces pale with disgust. I’m sure it would only be a matter of minutes until the cops showed up.

Jervis knelt beside Telixa’s lifeless torso, crying. I couldn’t believe the feelings were that real. As he continued to mourn, I surveyed the area, looking for clues that could give us some sense of direction.

“Jervis, there’s nothing here, man. We have to go. She’s gone,” I said, placing my hand on his shoulder.

“Yeah, I know. We have to find this guy,” Jervis replied.

“You mean Vinny?” a voice said through the crowd.

Sifting through the mass of onlookers, Jervis reached the person behind the voice. “Let’s go,” I heard him say as I started to backpedal. Finally, he emerged from the crowd with a young female who couldn’t have been any older than sixteen.

“She’s coming with us,” he said vehemently.

Now in the car, we pulled out just as the cops were pulling in.

"Jervis, who the fuck is this sixteen-year-old *runt*?" I asked, a mix of anger and confusion in my voice.

"You can ask me yourself. I am sitting right here," the pint-sized female Jervis had thrown in the back seat replied.

"Okay, well, who the fuck are you?" I snapped back.

"I'm Jessica, and Vinny was my friend. Also, for the record, I'm eighteen, not sixteen," she said, as if it was actually a big difference.

"Enough!" Jervis finally broke his silence. "Where is he?"

"Can we get something to eat first? I was about to leave to go get lunch when I saw that big ass commotion happening at the middle school. Obviously I'm nosey so I went to see what the deal was. I was barely there before your janky ass yanked me out." Jessica said, her arms crossed as she looked out the window.

Normally, Jervis would've flown off the handle at this sort of blatant defiance. Looking at him looking at her in the rearview, I understood. She was about 5'3", barely 100 pounds, with dark brown eyes and dark brown hair. However, the fact remained — this little *bitch* might actually know where the fuck Vinny was.

"Okay," I said loudly. "What the fuck? I mean, Telixa, goddamnit. Vinny was a weird motherfucker, but this shit… this is some whole other shit. What the fuck happened to this kid after we bounced from Florida?"

Jervis looked at me with rage in his eyes. "I don't know, Emerson, but I will tell you this: Vinny will pay for killing Telixa. This shit is fucking personal now." He motioned to Jessica. "Now start talking, *short stack*. What do you know?"

"Regency," she said, her voice steady. "Park by the food court entrance." She didn't offer any more information, instead pulling out her phone and tapping out a message as we drove.

Arriving at Regency Square, we parked where she had suggested and looked around. The silence in the car had been heavy, and watching her text, I had to assume she was setting up a meet.

"This is where he is?" Jervis asked. He looked skeptical. But this place did hold significance — a lot of fond memories.

"No... I just thought I knew someone here that could answer some of your questions," Jessica said.

We all sat there for a while with the engine running, silent. It was as if we were waiting for her to give us direction, and she was doing the same.

"All right, let's get on with it then," Emerson said as he and Jessica opened their doors and stepped out. I didn't. I rolled down the passenger-side window.

"Jessica, get in the driver's seat. We need to talk. Emerson, can you give us a minute?" I said. Me and Jervis were boys; nothing was secret. So I knew it wasn't anything personal he needed to speak with her about.

"Okay, man, I've been wanting to see that new *Benji Rodriguez* action flick for a minute," I said.

"Cool. Well, let me know how it goes," Jervis said, giving me the sacred shake.

"Likewise," I replied, moments before he began rolling up the tinted window.

A movie sounded good right about now, but after what happened, I couldn't relax. I scanned the area for anything that might connect this place to Vinny, but the scene was clean. No clues, no logic, nothing. Frustrated, I turned and started back toward the car where Jervis and Jessica were waiting.

"To be honest, Jervis, that was my cousin who was murdered at Eisenhower. I know you think I have answers, but I don't. That's why I was trying to bring you to someone that did," she said as she opened the driver's-side door, stepped out, and started to walk away.

As I got closer, I could see Jessica exiting the car. "Take care," she said with a smirk as she walked past me. I stood there for a few seconds, confused.

"Didn't we need her?" I asked.

Jervis didn't answer. He was staring past me, his face pale. "Emerson... we need to go. Now."

I turned and saw them — two figures stepping out from behind a pillar, both holding guns. The Regency parking lot suddenly felt like a cage. Jessica hadn't been a lead; she had been a lure.

Chapter 3 – The Council's Whisper

The screech of tires was the only answer I had for the two gunmen. Jervis slammed the gas, swinging the car around in a tight arc as the first shots cracked through the air, spider-webbing the rear windshield. We fishtailed out of the parking lot, the image of those two figures shrinking in the rearview mirror. My heart was still hammering against my ribs minutes later when we finally pulled into the relative safety of a gas station on the other side of town. Jervis killed the engine, and the sudden silence was deafening.

"So, Emerson, what do you think?" Jervis asked, his voice low and ragged.

"Well, I say we hit the library and start looking up articles on all the local killings. I've got a feeling he's killed more people than what's being reported. He had to have started somewhere, so I say we go there. And the video store, of course."

Ah, the video store. Amidst all this craziness, we hadn't even followed up on our first lead. But next stop was the public library. I figured we'd get what we could out of here, and then it was down to the video store.

I can't believe we're back here. Riverview. Jervis was the first to enter the library. I fell back so I could check my messages on the new phone I bought just before this nonsense began. Lisa, Angela, Pamela, Renee… I really didn't want to talk to any of them. So, I ignored the whole lot and proceeded to the entrance. Once inside, I noticed Jervis already scanning the microfiche for clues.

"How far back are you going?" I asked.

"Five months. I know his murders don't go that far back, but maybe we can find the actual lighter that lit this fuse," Jervis replied.

Jervis was always that way — a chess mindset. Thinking ahead. In this case, backwards. And while he continued to absorb the local events of the past five months, I went over to chat with a familiar *bird* I spotted.

"Selina, Selina," I said as I approached a Rubenesque, high-yellow *bird*.

"It's *Sexy Red*, fool!" she said as she jumped out of her seat to give me a hug. We sat down and began to catch up.

"How have you been?" I asked as I sat down next to her.

"I'm good. What are you doing here?" she asked.

"Vinny. We're trying to locate him. Those killings that's been going on, we think it's him, seriously," I said.

She looked down, started grinding her teeth. Her eyes got watery. What was this? I asked myself.

She looked up, and with a firm voice, she said, "Leave. This ain't the place for you."

"What are you talking about?" I replied as Jervis joined us at the table.

"He works for *C.O.K.E.*," she said.

We looked at her with disbelief. "Are you freaking kidding me? What the fuck does his job at Coca-Cola have to do with him killing folks?" Jervis asked.

"*C.O.K.E.*, it's an acronym," she said.

"An acronym for what?" I replied.

She sat up straight, looked intensely into my eyes, and said, "The *Council of Kill 'Em*."

Immediately, we both looked at each other and laughed. She didn't like that very much.

"You fools have no idea what you got yourselves into. See, you left and have been gone for a long time. These people — if that's what you want to call them — have had a tight control over this town for years now, and your boy Vinny is just what they needed to…" She stopped mid-sentence and just collapsed. No blood or anything, just hit the floor.

"Jervis, what the fuck is going on here?"

"I have no idea, man, but we need to call an ambulance and get the fuck out of here."

The librarian came running with her cell phone when I yelled, "Get an ambulance!" I grabbed the can of Coke that was on the table she was sitting at. I figured whatever did this to *Sexy Red* must have been in the Coke can.

Jetting out of the library and jumping into the car, we sat there. Knowing the cop's where undoubtedly close to arriving, we sat there. We just needed a beat to collect our thoughts.

"Well, Emerson, this is really getting interesting. Isn't it funny that we just want to keep getting deeper into this without the fear of getting killed?" Jervis asked.

"Actually, look how efficient and methodical Vinny has been. He's killed everyone we've talked to. If he really wanted us dead, I think he could have pulled it off by now, no problem," I said, realizing what I'd just admitted. Yeah, he could have killed us at any time.

"Yeah, you're right. So, the Coke can you grabbed — it killed her. Let's go find out if that's true and take it to Bliz."

Bliz. Wow, it's been a while since I heard that name. Donald Stokley, aka *Blizid*, was a close friend of ours until we grew apart. Now, Bliz is one of the best chemists in the world, and if anyone was going to tell us what was in this Coke can, Bliz would be our best bet.

"Right. But first things first, though. The video store."

Chapter 4 – Souvenir In the Tailpipe

Turning down Boyette Road. Memories all around us — some good, some bad. A lot happened around these parts. We could've just gone down Riverview Drive; it would've been quicker. I guess Jervis wanted to go the long way down memory lane.

Post office on the left, Riverview High on the right. We finally reached the Publix shopping center where Hollywood Video is located.

As we're turning in, our eyes glance to the left, across the street. *BP*. A gas station. Its name has been changed, but it will always be *BP* to us. Nothing crazy ever really happened there; it was just the centerpiece to the chaotic puzzle we were putting together as kids. No time for nostalgia, though. We've got a job to do.

Walking into the video store, not sure where to start looking, we just wandered for a while, piecing together what we'd been able to ascertain so far.

"This guy is nuts, Emerson. And he might not have even been here lately. Plus, I highly doubt there's anyone on staff from back when he frequented this joint," Jervis said, rather deflated.

"I'm still here!" someone yelled from the next aisle over. It had to be a short cat because the Betamax racks weren't that high. Then, from around the corner… *Hussle*.

"What up?" he said as he walked around the corner.

"Hey. I thought you were out in New York doing your rap thing?" Jervis said in a sarcastic tone, which of course, *Hussle* didn't pick up on.

"Man, I was, but they wasn't respecting my flow. I think my hot lyrics intimidated them, honestly. My *16's* had them shook. I'm telling you; I got that fire. They just don't know, man. They just don't know."

Jervis bent down to tie his shoes so *Hussle* wouldn't see him laughing. I had to stop the madness, and I did so by switching the subject to something relevant and real.

"So you worked here when Vinny used to come around?" I asked.

"Yeah, I did, but his whole vibe was something creepy. He was mad quiet, never really talked to anyone. I heard he could flow, but he would never spit," *Hussle* replied.

"Well, just be lucky that your ass is still alive," Jervis interjected.

"Huh?" *Hussle* said, confused.

"Never mind. It's good to see you, man, but we gotta get out of here. There is nothing here for us," Jervis said in a rush.

So, it didn't pan out the way we were hoping it would. Big deal. We still had Bliz and the Coke can. Speaking of which, I had developed quite a thirst. As we were walking out of the video store, I started to turn around to go back in.

"Where you going, Emerson?"

I started to laugh a little due to the earlier situation with the Coke can and said, "I'm thirsty, bro. I'm grabbing a Coke."

Jervis stood outside while I ran in quickly. *Hussle* had to be in the back because I didn't see him anywhere. I grabbed the Coke and yelled out, "Yo, *Hussle*, come ring me up for this Coke."

No response. I waited two minutes. He could have been in the bathroom or something, but five went by, and nothing. No, not again, I thought, and started walking to the back.

As I made my way there, Jervis walked in with a look on his face like, What the hell is taking you so long? I motioned for him to follow me in the back and shot him a look like something was wrong.

We got to the back and found nothing except a stack of CDs in front of the bathroom door, and the back door of the store was wide open with a trash bag blocking the hallway.

"Okay, let's see what's behind door number one," Jervis said.

I opened the bathroom door, but there was no sign of *Hussle*.

Leaving the bathroom, me and Emerson were about to continue looking when I realized something.

"Do we really care?" I asked. Emerson gave me a what the fuck look. "*Hussle* — do we really care if he got his *lights turned off*? I mean, with all due disrespect, he was a douche," I continued.

Emerson didn't say a word, just shrugged as we turned to exit the building, grabbing the surveillance tape on our way out. No, we didn't do anything illegal, but we ain't got time to be explaining all that to the law if something actually did happen to *Hussle*.

"All right, Jervis, let's jet," I said as I put the car in reverse. Guess I should've checked the rearview first. A bump. Then… thump-scrape-grind. A loud noise came from underneath the car as I backed up.

Not really caring to figure out who or what it was at that particular time, I sped off. And in less than a minute, we were deep into the winding roads of a subdivision called Riverglen. We pulled into a little park located at the back of the subdivision to eye the damage.

Getting out of the car, I started to get a little curious. What did I run over?

Once we got to the back of the car, we were shocked. Stuffed in the tailpipe was curly hair. Familiar curly hair. *Hussle*'s. What the fuck was he doing behind us?

"We have to get the entire outer body disinfected, especially underneath," Jervis said.

"Bet. I'll hit up *Crazy Legs*," I replied.

Chapter 5 – The Mouth of the Storm

Not only did *Crazy Legs* fix the *whip*, but she gave us a new one to boot — an old favor she'd owed for some time now. To tell the truth, I had completely forgotten about it until she brought it up. We drove back to the hotel to recap the day and plan what we were going to do next. When we arrived at the room, there was a letter lying on the floor. Jervis picked it up quickly and began to open it.

He started reading:

"Leave now. Leave this town, for you do not know the dangers that lie ahead. This is much deeper than you can imagine. If you do not leave, you will be killed and made an example. You have been warned."

We looked at each other like, Yeah, right. This can't be real.

"After all the deaths today and all the craziness, did they really think that a letter was going to stop us? Really? A fucking letter?" I yelled.

Jervis just shook his head. "Okay, first thing tomorrow, we'll go see Bliz and find out what's in this Coke can. I have a feeling it's going to tell us a lot more than we think."

Bliz had once been a good friend, and we would have liked to see him under better circumstances — but as they say, *it is what it is*.

When I woke up, Jervis was already up watching the news. Fortunately, the cops had no info on who or what we looked like. There were no witnesses at the video store to even confirm we were there, so for the time being, they were pinning this one on Vinny as well. They still couldn't figure out his real name or any info on him — which, I figured, you could thank the *Council of Kill 'Em* for. So for now, he was being dubbed *"The Black Squall"* — the media's way of saying he hit like a sudden Florida storm, fast and violent, leaving nothing but wreckage in his wake.

I mean, the whole concept of giving a serial killer a celebrity-like name was idiotic and, if anything, probably made the bastard want to kill more. You're practically making the sick fuck a TV star.

But nobody saw it that way — except for Jervis. He thought all serial killers, rapists, and so on who gained large media attention were celebritized in a way. I remember him telling me that murder was the same thing as murder. He said, "I once watched a shitty B-movie for fifteen minutes, and I swear to Allah it made me want to slit my wrists with rusty nails. How is that any different from someone begging to die because they're being tortured by some sick fuck that got beat by his dad and ignored by his older brother growing up?"

Good point, I thought.

"Emerson, let's go. We've got to meet Bliz at his lab in Tropical Acres in twenty-two minutes," I said.

Emerson was moving sluggishly this morning. No pep. He needed coffee. Hell, I needed coffee. So, while Emerson got dressed, I was finna head to the mess hall to get us some chow and strong coffee. I grabbed the handle, paused. I stepped on something. Another note. It read:

"Next stop, *T-Dot*."

I knew what the note meant. Someone sacred to the circle was being targeted, someone so sacred we never even mentioned their name. The game had changed. We were just going to try to talk Vinny down, but now the die was cast.

"Emerson, here," I said, passing him the note.

Ever since we got back into town, we'd been hearing that *Dot* was visiting for a few days before heading back to Canada. We didn't try to look for *Dot* because we didn't want to get sidetracked — among other unspoken reasons. Now, we had to play protector for two days until *Dot* got on that plane.

Still staring at the note, Emerson said, "We can't let *Dot* know we're watching her. We just have to keep watch and protect her."

Protect her. The words echoed in my head as I pulled onto the highway. It was one thing to hunt a killer, but another entirely to become a shadow — a guardian angel for someone who couldn't know we existed. The whole thing felt impossible.

Finally, on our way to see Bliz. We were somewhat late, but oh well. I drove because I knew Jervis's mind was elsewhere.

"Emerson, this is bad. This is beyond crossing the line. This is crucifying-Jesus kind of bad," I said.

Emerson just nodded. He knew what was up. What was Vinny thinking? He knew the deal. He knew who *Dot* was. He knew who *Dot* was to me. He knew who *Dot* was to us. Was he suicidal? I had to push those thoughts back for now; we'd arrived at Bliz's.

Bliz seemed happy to see us, but he was being really anal about the time and us being late. I thought nothing of it. Time is a thief that leaves nothing behind — so right now, time was not our friend by any means. I explained the situation to Bliz, and for some reason, I noticed a weird kind of look on his face after mentioning C.O.K.E.

No way, I thought. Bliz too?

I shot a look at Jervis, and it was clear he was thinking the same thing. But for now, let's pump whatever info we can on the substance in the Coke can. Bliz came out of the lab with a look of confusion on his face.

"Whatever was in this Coke can did not kill Selina, guys. This is nothing but flat Coca-Cola."

Damn, I thought. The only freaking lead we had left. Then it hit me.

"That's great, Bliz, but I never mentioned Selina's name."

Bliz didn't even blink. He just pulled out some kind of weapon — we couldn't even tell what the damn thing was — and started swinging. We moved out of the way and subdued him pretty easily.

"Wow, Bliz, really? You too?" Jervis said as we held him down. I found some rope in his lab to tie him up with.

"You guys just don't get it. You came back to this town, and now you have no way out. You're stuck, just like the rest of us. It's only a matter of time before Vinny gets you guys. I tried to get you out of here with no harm, but you had to be slick. Fuck it, none of this matters. We are all dead anyway."

This was starting to get way out of hand — and a lot deeper than we had anticipated.

"Well, Jervis, what do you wanna do now?" I asked, not really sure what to do about Bliz.

"This all seems like a bad episode of *The Twilight Zone,* man. The only thing we can do is get out of here. Killing Bliz is not an option, though he did try to hurt us."

Then Bliz yelled out, "I didn't want to! They threatened my family, man! My family! What was I supposed to do?" Then he started convulsing, foam spilling from his mouth. His head just dropped, and he was gone. Most likely a tiny cyanide pill in a false tooth. Guess that was his final act of protecting his family. Once C.O.K.E. finds him like this, I figure they'll reckon he killed himself rather than talk.

"You have to be kidding me. This can't be happening again, man," Jervis said.

"No time to talk about it, kid. We have to make moves. I'm sure whoever was pulling Bliz's strings probably has someone coming by to check on what's happened to us," I responded.

Then a walkie-talkie went off in the room.

"Donald, report. What is the status?"

I grabbed it quickly. "Nothing as of yet. They're still late and have not shown up," I said, muffling my voice to disguise it. That ought to buy us some time to get out of here, at least.

"We're keeping this thing. We might get some kind of lead as to what we can do next," I said.

"And just what do we do next, Emerson?" asked Jervis.

"Good question, Jervis. Good question."

Chapter 6 – Solar System Beyond Rage

Out of everyone who had died thus far, Bliz was the hardest pill to swallow. With no real leads to go on, the only thing me and Jervis could do for the time being was to be *Dot's angels*. Our *local ear* told us that Dot would be watching a movie at Regency at 12:30. I looked at the time on my cell: 1:47. The movie should be over soon. Apparently, Jervis was thinking the same thing; he was already hitting the on-ramp headed for Brandon. I'm glad we were taking the car *Crazy Legs* gave us because she also supplied a trunk full of goodies, including disguises.

"All right, Emerson, you ready for this?" Jervis asked as he pulled into the parking lot.

"No. But what choice do we have?" I replied.

He popped the trunk, then we walked to the back of the car. "Wow," I said. The trunk was littered with bats, pipes, brass knuckles, pig's feet, masks, wigs, fake mustaches, and Cracker Jacks. We knew we didn't have much time, so we pretty much threw on the first things we grabbed. Jervis looked like a *post-Richard Pryor*, and I looked like a *Mexican landscaper* who'd had some hard living.

"Let's head to the shop next to the theater," I said to Emerson as I closed the trunk.

When we got to the shop, people were already pouring out of the theater. Could this be Dot's group letting out? Before I could even ask the question aloud…

"There's Dot," Emerson said quietly.

"All right, all right. Be cool. Let's try to blend in and keep a safe distance," I replied.

We stayed about four people back. It was kind of funny; we were standing directly behind an old man with Alzheimer's who had written down a reminder to beat his wife in a tiny notebook because she'd fallen asleep during the movie. Anyway, Dot was getting in the car. We had to rush to ours because it was hella far from where Dot had parked. Emerson took the wheel and began weaving gracefully through the parking lot until we were in sight of Dot's car.

So far, so good. Nothing out of the ordinary was going on; it didn't look like any of the cars around us were following her. Still, I clocked a black van idling two rows over, engine running. Probably nothing — but it stuck in my head. We trailed Dot to a house in Apollo Beach. Man, I fucking hated this place. Not only did the beach suck, but the town itself really had nothing to offer. It was one of those towns you roll through to get to the next town and never think about again.

"Well shit, man, I really don't want to just sit out here on some *Richard Dreyfuss–Emilio Estevez type shit*," I said, getting aggravated. One thing I hated was sitting somewhere for an extended period of time doing absolutely nothing.

"Look, man, you know I can't have anything happen to Dot. Dot is my li— It just can't happen," Jervis said, a little worried. He never really gets rattled like that, and already knowing how important she was to him, I gave him the nod of recognition.

"Okay, Jervis, it's getting dark. I figure if these *cats* are going to make a move, they would do it by now," I said, scanning the area. I began to think to myself — would they send Valducci to do the deed? I mean, they have to know we have eyes on her after sending us the note and all, right?

"I know talking to Vinny was the initial plan, but at this point, I'm ready to kill this fucker," I mentioned to Jervis as I saw him pointing to something.

"You mean that fucker?"

And there he was — Valducci — walking up the driveway like it was the right thing to do. I was about to bolt out of the car like a madman when Jervis stopped me. I was the *bull of the bunch,* often running into situations with a head of steam and asking questions later. Jervis was a little more methodical with his actions.

"What the fu—" I was interrupted.

"Shh, man. Something doesn't look right. Just hold up a second."

We watched Vinny walk up to the front door. The front door? Really? I was floored. Shit, we both were. Dot opened the door — not with a look of *Who the fuck is this at my door?* but with a look like she was happy to see Vinny. And then they started kissing.

I quickly turned to see if Jervis was about to flip, but he spoke very calmly. "This is what they wanted us to see. Killing Dot was never the intention. They wanted to break us. She is clearly under their control. This is a lot worse than I had thought."

Emerson had the right thought initially. We needed to rush 'em. I know this started off about Vinny, but apparently, there is a larger picture, and I planned on stealing and breaking it. Like Bane did to Batman, but more vicious. Furthermore, we didn't need Vinny to play the lead. That was *our* role. And because of that, he became irrelevant.

"Promise me you'll take her to the airport," I said to Emerson.

"Now? But what about…" he stopped mid-sentence. He already knew the answer to the question he didn't even finish asking.

"Her flight isn't until tomorrow… Fuck it, I got connections. I'll get her on the first flight to Canada. You sure you want to do this, though? Once you pop a balloon, it's popped," Emerson continued.

"Right now, it's not about C.O.K.E. Yeah, they were the ones who put the sword in his hands, but the choice was his, and he chose to cut my heart out with it. There's no going back. Just get her on that plane, then come scoop me," I replied.

Emerson looked a little confused and said, "Pick you up from where? Here? Tampa International is like an hour away. It's really going to take you two hours?"

I just nodded as we began walking toward the front door without ever discussing a plan of attack. We were in sync. I waited at the front door as Emerson kicked it in and rushed toward the moans.

"What the fuck, man!" Vinny yelled.

Then I heard the crashing of glass. I assumed it was Vinny's body being tossed through something because immediately after that, I heard Emerson yell, "STAY YOUR *FUNKY ASS* DOWN, YOU *CHEWY BASTARD*!"

I then heard him telling Dot to get dressed. Moments later, another sound of breaking glass.

"I TOLD YOUR *CHEWY ASS* TO STAY DOWN, YOU *FUNKY BASTARD*!" Emerson yelled.

I didn't even once think of heading in there prematurely. I knew Emerson had the *sitch* handled.

"They said they would kill Jervis if I didn't *scrump* Vinny!" Dot cried out through the commotion.

Hearing that, I started to grind my teeth. Then, walking out of the front door, were Dot and Emerson. Dot reached out to embrace me, but I turned away. My emotions weren't in the joyous range at that particular point in time. Actually, there isn't even a word that has ever been written in any language that could explain how I was feeling right then. I was an entire solar system beyond rage.

I watched as Emerson and Dot got into the car and sped off. Now, it was my turn.

I walked in just as he finished dressing. Before he could speak or react, I rushed him, slamming his head against the wall. I stepped back as he fell to the ground, holding his head.

"Not cool, man!" he said.

He opened his mouth to speak again, but before he could, I kicked his jaw — hard. He fell onto his side with blood and teeth leaking from his mouth.

"That's just the appetizer," I said as I grabbed him by the back of the neck as if he were a kitten and dragged him into the dining room, duct-taping him to the table. No longer were there words coming out of his mouth, just a stream of gushing blood. I paused for a second, thinking of the old Kung Fu movies where they'd slice a limb off with a sword and blood would gush. I must have thought too hard because I didn't realize he'd wiggled free and managed to grab a little statue or something and nailed me in the head with it. He got to his feet and began to say something.

"Hold on, you fucking maniac, no you don't."

That was enough for me. My whole body was completely consumed with a blood rage that rivaled a dwarven warrior on battle day. I tackled him to the ground, mounted his chest, and began pummeling the son of a bitch until he no longer resisted. As he lay there, stewing in his own blood, I stood up and admired my work — probably like Picasso would have after he had just painted a masterpiece.

Never being one to stop there, I told Vinny, "We haven't even begun to have fun yet, you sick bastard. You think what you have done is sick? I'm going to show you some pain."

I went to the kitchen and quickly grabbed what I was looking for: a butcher knife, a cheese grinder, and a turkey baster. The spot where that bastard hit me felt like it was pulsating and was probably bleeding, but it made no difference. To think we were going to talk to this guy… but the only person this *cat* was talking to was whoever was waiting on the other side.

The thoughts in my head were no longer of a worldly nature. I felt like one of those villains in the movies who gets that sensational rush right before they do their dastardly deed.

I started to make my way back to the dining room and heard broken glass. Vinny had jumped through the window and was dashing down the street. I started after him, but a black van pulled up beside him. He jumped in, and it was gone.

Chapter 7 – Casualties Happen

I grabbed my cell phone and tried to call Emerson, who should be at the airport by now.

I was racing at full speed, convinced that there had to be someone tailing us. One thing was on my mind: get Dot the fuck out of here and get back to Jervis.

"I am so sorry! They made me! I had to, I had to, Emerson!" A sobbing Dot went to speak again, but I interjected.

"Dot, this is very important. Trust me, I understand what you went through is crazy, but I need you to get it together and listen. Jervis wants me to take you to the airport, but I can't do that. These *C.O.K.E.* people have a vast influence, and I'm sure it reaches the airport. So, I'm going to send you on the Greyhound."

I was calm but extremely worried for Jervis. I knew he could handle his own, but what if Vinny wasn't alone? The thought made me want to turn around, but I stayed on course.

"Okay, we're here. I need you to get on that bus. Only you're not going home. Toronto, yes, but you're going to stay with a friend until we get this mess sorted out."

When we first got into the car, Dot was in a state of shock, and I had phoned an old friend who owed us a favor. He had enough connections to keep Dot safe and unfound. Who knew if *C.O.K.E.* reached that far or not, but for right now, I trusted Kevin — and so did Jervis — so I already knew he'd be cool with it.

Right after I dropped off Dot and made sure she was safe, I got back in the car, and my phone began to ring. I picked up quickly, seeing that it was Jervis.

"Tell me that *bitch* is dead," I said, but something told me I already knew the answer.

"He got away," Jervis said.

"How'd he get away? Are you okay?" I asked.

"I'm fine. And I let him. Get Dot gone and meet me at *BP* in two hours," he replied before hanging up.

I knew Emerson was confused, but I wasn't. When I first laid hands on that *sick bastard,* I placed a tracker underneath his collar. I wanted to take out as many *C.O.K.E. products* as I could. I really did want to torture him first before letting him escape, but oh well.

As soon as I hung up with Emerson, I saw a young girl approaching in a small sports car with an older gentleman in the passenger seat. It was a residential neighborhood, so they were rolling slowly. Right behind me were two boys, no older than eleven or twelve, holding skateboards and talking about Pokémon.

Once the car got in close enough proximity, I took action. In a singular motion, I spun around 180 degrees and grabbed the closest boy. By the time I hit 360, his head hit the driver's side window, shattering it. I threw him to the concrete, then punched and pulled the young girl through the shattered window and placed her in the same spot before hopping in the car and speeding off.

The elderly gentleman was frozen. I broke the silence. "So, who was that chick? She was one *hot piece*," I said.

"She—she—sh—she's my daughter. I was teaching her how to drive," he stammered.

Trying to lighten the mood, I chuckled. "Well, you should've been teaching her how to take a punch. That *bitch's* jaw is weak."

He didn't laugh. Why didn't he laugh? That was pretty funny. Anyway, I pulled out my phone and opened the tracking app. To my surprise, they were close — parked in a private garage. Hidden, but not far. I parked a block away and surveyed the area.

"Thanks for the ride. And here's my number. Tell your daughter to hit me up when she gets out of the hospital," I said, stepping out. The father slid into the driver's seat and calmly drove off. He seemed nice, considering. Wait — I needed him. I flagged him down before he got too far.

"I need one thing from you and I'm out of your life, I promise," I said, leaning in close and whispering the plan. A normal person might've driven off. Must've been the shock. Whatever the reason, he nodded.

I then walked up to the garage, standing just to the right of it, waiting. I heard tires screeching. It was the father. He came flying down the street, ramming his already damaged vehicle through the front of the garage and out the back. He never stopped, just continued down the backstreet, disappearing into the traffic.

That whole stunt was just to gain entrance, but it ended up solving both of my problems. All of the henchmen were on the ground, twitching, barely able to move. Broken bones aplenty. Vinny Valducci got the worst of it. You could visibly see the tire tracks on his face. His sternum was damn near touching his back. Not by my hands, but good enough.

"I have protection, people who'll look after me. I'll be okay. Tell Jervis… you know," Dot said before boarding the bus that would take her far from this madness.

My phone blared as soon as I sped off. "What's the deal, *playboy*?" It was Jervis. Plans had changed.

"Riverglen. I got five of them, including Vinny, on the ground right now."

No more needed to be said. I was on my way, smoking a doobie and excited about getting to the scene. The vision was clear in my head: five of them. Jervis must be having a blast. I needed to hurry the fuck up before I missed out on all the fun, so I jumped on the crosstown, which should knock about twenty to thirty minutes off my route. The crosstown had changed a lot since we used to ride it; lanes were wider, and the traffic was still nonexistent, so it didn't take long to get to my destination.

I pulled up to Riverglen. As I rolled past the park, I noticed three cars parked there, but I saw no one in the park. As soon as I passed, they moved in pursuit. Unfortunately for them, I already had a sinister smile and a plan.

I pulled up to Hussle's block. Why not maximize efficiency? Jervis was just the next block over. Hussle was a *punk* from our high school days I never got to deal with. And even though *C.O.K.E.* most likely had the police on lock, we were in *"anything goes"* territory.

The plan was simple. Me and Jervis had placed a bomb under the car in case of an emergency, each with a detonator linked to our phones. When they pulled up to confront me in Hussle's driveway — boom. Wipe out Hussle's house and the neighbors. Sucks for them, but casualties happen. One innocent family is nothing compared to the whole town. Hell, they were probably brainwashed anyway.

The only thing was to make sure Hussle was home and his two shitty-ass parents were there for the fireworks. I sped up a little but left enough space to make sure they knew where I was going. When I pulled up in the driveway, the garage door was open. This was too perfect. Not only did this mean they were home, but I could also plant the car in the garage and cause maximum damage.

I pulled into the garage and left the car running. As they pulled into the driveway, I burst into Hussle's living room. The whole family was there watching TV. When they saw me, they were shocked, and they didn't move. I jumped through the sliding glass door in the back and ran through the backyard. As I turned around before hopping his neighbor's fence, I noticed that the henchmen had made their way into Hussle's living room, and the family was pointing me out to them. Those bastards, I thought to myself. I'm really going to love this.

As soon as I cleared the fence, I hit the detonator and dove into the neighbor's pool.

"Grab my hand," I said to Emerson as I walked up to the pool. He grabbed hold, and I pulled him out.

"That was sweet, man. I just blew up Hussle, his *fam*, some *C.O.K.E. characters*, and a couple of parrots," Emerson said, grinning.

I paused, confused. "Sorry to break it to you, man, but Hussle was already dead. Remember? We ran over him the other day. His hair was in our tailpipe, for Christ's sake. Ringing any bells?"

Emerson actually had to think about it. Then I realized he was high.

"Look, man, this mission requires a clear head. That's it — no more smoking," I said sternly.

"Okay, okay. Where do we go from here? What's next?" Emerson asked.

"The next step is you going back to the hotel to chill and clear your head. I'm heading back to Eisenhower to figure some things out," I replied. We nodded, then went our separate ways.

Chapter 8 – Step One, Complete

It didn't take me long to get back to the school, which was almost out. As soon as that bell rang, I went class to class, talking to teachers, posing as a journalist, trying to find out anything pertaining to *C.O.K.E.* I had to be subtle — I couldn't just outright ask about a killer organization.

When talking to one of the teachers, I noticed she was wearing a ring that looked familiar. I couldn't place it at first. She was going on about the Telixa tragedy, but my mind was elsewhere. Where had I seen that ring? Then it hit me — at the garage where Emerson took out all of those *agents*. Before I left the scene, I went inside to witness the carnage. I only remembered the ring because one of the *agent's* arms had been ripped clean from its socket and was lying about two or three feet from him. And even though I didn't have an audience, I couldn't resist making a joke at that point — I walked over to the detached arm, bent down, and checked for a pulse.

Standing before the teacher, I literally laughed out loud at the memory. She stopped talking mid-sentence.

"Are you sick?" she asked.

"Huh? What do you mean?" I replied.

She put down the coffee mug she was holding, folded her arms, and said, "Well, I was talking about Telixa being mutilated, and you started laughing."

"No, no, no. I wasn't paying attention to you. I was chuckling about something that happened earlier. But staying on the subject of mutilation, how about you tell me about *C.O.K.E.* before I break that coffee mug on the floor and rub your fat face in it?" I said calmly.

She looked shocked. She didn't know what to do, so I helped her along. I picked up the coffee mug and dropped it on the floor. It shattered.

"Step one, complete. Do you really want to move on to step two?" I asked.

She looked down and shook her head. We sat down, and she spilled everything she knew.

"Look, I don't know what *C.O.K.E.* is now; I just know what it used to be," she said.

"And what did it used to be?" I asked.

"It used to be a way to stop the nonsense. I mean, it was just a group of guys pretty much being vigilantes of some sort. Like, if someone was being ignorant and loud just because they were in a long line at a grocery store, they would get stabbed in the neck. Or if some black guy with his pants drooping down to his kneecaps walked into McDonald's and asked for a Whopper, they'd cut off his nipples and sew them to his eyes, then break his spine. I remember when one of the *C.O.K.E.* members worked at a deli, and some black guy hopped up on marijuana bought a roast beef sandwich. He then complained that there was not enough roast beef in the sandwich. Understandable. Everyone complains sometimes. But what wasn't understandable or acceptable was him getting belligerent. The *C.O.K.E.* member was calm and offered him a refund. It didn't matter. This guy was gone. So the C.O.K.E. member leaped over the counter and stabbed the black guy 333 times. Then he cut up the body, mixed it with some other meat, and fed it to the customers. He gave the bones to his dog. His mindset was that *any* ridiculousness would result in death — no exceptions," she continued.

This *bitch* had to be crazy. She was obviously feeding me some horseshit that was probably partly true, which only made me happy because now it was on to step two. I locked her in the closet of the classroom when I was done and made my way back to the hotel.

That's it. I'm done blazing till we get home. I really thought I saw Hussle in that living room. It must have been his cousin or something. It didn't matter; he was still family, so he deserved to die. I wonder if Jervis got any leads. It was still dark in the room when I finally got myself to bed. I flipped on the TV when the news started talking about a teacher found in the classroom closet with her face mutilated. I shook my head. Jervis was at it again. These *C.O.K.E.* bastards really had no idea who they were fucking with. In one day, the two of us managed to take out a plethora of their people, and we had only just begun.

As I got up to go to the bathroom to flush the rest of my herb, I noticed another letter under the door. Here we go again, I thought. But before I could pick it up, Jervis busted through the door.

"Good job on the teacher. Way to go *lo-pro*," I said, laughing a little.

"She had it coming, man. She was *C.O.K.E.* and a lying *cunt* at that," he chuckled.

"Yeah, I figured that as well, but look, we got another letter."

Jervis bent down and picked it up.

"So what does it say?" I asked with anticipation.

"It just says '*Linger*.' It's from Dot. Her way of letting me know we're good," he said.

Emerson just shook his head as we walked out the door, heading to the parking lot. We were pretty much out of clues. All we knew was that we wanted to open up the Council's chest and rip its heart out. That business with Dot sealed their fate.

"We're out of clues, man," Jervis said.

"No, we're not," Emerson replied as he pulled out his cell and started going through it.

"Who are you texting? This has been a long day, and I'm not really down for anything extra," Jervis added.

Jervis started going through his phone book in his mind. Who could he be reaching out to? Everyone we knew had either been killed, gone missing, or was choosing to be unreachable.

"Got it. Head to Captain Jack's," Emerson blurted out.

Not good. That place was watched heavily by the cops. Their boy Lopez from years back used to work there and would give illegal immigrants jobs. Even after he left, the staff continued the tradition. It seemed like a van full of Mexicans was being escorted out of there every night by the police. And after all the carnage we'd bestowed upon the town, the police were the last people on earth we wanted to see. But Emerson had a lead — our only lead. We had to follow up.

We weren't far; we got there in no time. Glancing around, I saw cops on all sides. We had to be cool. We got out of the car and went in. Drunken, toothless bodies at every table, it seemed.

"Okay, Emerson, who the fuck are we here to…" Before I could finish the sentence, I saw him. Marcus.

"What up, guys?" he said as he gave us both the standard pound and half-hug.

I looked at Emerson with a menacing scowl. He looked back at me with an it's-him-or-no-one look. He was right; we needed a lead. Bad. We all sat down, and I cut right through the bullshit.

"Look, me and Jervis need some info on—"

"The *Council*," Marcus interjected. "Small town, remember. Listen, you might be able to get to the *embryos*, but you'll never get to the *ovary*," he continued. Marcus always had a crazy way of saying shit. Nevertheless, we had to find something out, so we had to entertain this clown.

"Well, give me a starting point, Marcus. There has to be someone or something that can lead us down the right path." I truly hated this fucking guy, and the sad part was I really didn't have a reason to. I mean, he had never really done anything messed up to me; I just didn't like the way the guy was.

"Well, I do know a spot you can go to that will probably lead you somewhere. Old stomping grounds, Déjà Vu. They pretty much got a lock on all the whores in this town, and their main one works at Déjà Vu. So, if anything, right there is where you can find something out. Her name is *Miracle*, but you need to be careful. She is one of them, man. I've only survived this long by keeping my mouth shut and pretty much looking the other way. By the way, you should leave. They got people coming to get you very soon. I would use the back door. Take my keys and give me yours."

Marcus was helping us a little too much, and I wanted to question it, but if he was right and they were on their way, we had to make moves. We made our way out and jumped in Marcus's car. I couldn't get it out of my head.

"Jervis, don't you think Marcus was a little too nice? I mean, they turned Bliz against us, man, and Marcus was never really a friend of ours."

Jervis looked at me like, what else were we supposed to do?

"I hear you, Emerson, but what were we supposed to do? I mean, if they were coming, we had to avoid a scene. The *bobbies* were all over the place."

He was right. Really, there wasn't much we could do. Still, I wasn't comfortable, so I pulled over at the first huge parking lot we saw, and we hotwired another car, leaving Marcus's there.

Chapter 9 – Two Cokes on the Rocks

Emerson was right; something about Marcus's story didn't smell right. But we had to get out of there. Now we were in a *jacked* vehicle on our way to a *whorehouse*.

"The *main man* must be pretty powerful," I started to say to Emerson. He just nodded. Then I asked, "Do you think it's someone we know?"

"I doubt it. Pretty much everyone we know around these parts are *low-budget cats,*" Emerson said.

He was right. We didn't know too many people with the know-how or ambition to pull off such intricate moves. Before the *convo* could continue, we made it.

"All right, Jervis, let's see what's going on in here," I said, stepping out of the car. Emerson looked a little preoccupied. I wasn't. I was focused.

As we walked through the doors, it all came back to me — that familiar smell. A mixture of hair spray, *coochie*, beer, shame, and desperation.

"Hey, barkeep, two Cokes on the rocks," I said as we bellied up to the bar. We had our backs to the stage because I wanted to eat at some point, and a *C-section scar party* would've ruined my appetite.

When the barkeep brought our drinks, I asked, "Which one is Miracle?"

"*Miracle Whip* isn't here. She got arrested earlier. Charged with murder, if you can believe it," he said with a hearty chuckle.

Me and Emerson looked at each other in disbelief. So much death. I pulled out my cell to check *the wire*, to see if her foolishness had hit *the line* yet. Jackpot. Emerson scooted closer as I started reading the report out loud.

"Today, a young woman only identified as *Miracle Whip* went into work today at The Dollar Tree, probably thinking it would be a normal day. It wasn't. Midway through her shift working as a cashier, a customer came through her line bringing with them fifty items. After ringing everything up, she gave the customer the total. The customer then motioned for a friend who was standing right outside looking in the window to come in. The friend came in with a huge duffel bag filled with pennies. Taking them out of the bag one by one, the customer began counting. According to an eyewitness, once the customer had gotten to $2.13, Miracle had enough. She pulled out a small pistol and before the customer could get to $2.15, her brain and the candy on the shelf directly behind her became one. Miracle did not try to flee. Instead, she sat on top of a nearby counter and waited for the police while repeating the phrase, 'That bitch should not have tried me.' Police arrived and took her to Orient County Jail, where she currently remains as of this broadcast."

I put away my phone, and we both just sat back, wondering where we go from here. I threw a twenty on the bar to pay for the Cokes as we got up to leave.

"Hey, I heard you were asking about my girl, *Mir,*" a *bottom-heavy stripper* said as she walked up to us with her hand on her hip.

"Uh, yeah," I said, looking out the corner of my eye at Emerson.

"Well, if you want info, then you gotta spend some," she said, obviously referring to one of us paying her for a private dance.

"Jervis, you have to take this bullet. The smell of prostitution is making me nauseous," Emerson said as he backpedaled toward the exit.

"Okay, man, but you owe me," I hollered back as the stripper grabbed me by the hand and led me to a dingy room in the back.

I have to get the hell out of here before I hurl. I don't see one *fine bird* in this whole place. Plus the Coke is flat. It's just horrible. But *Miracle,* that shit's funny. Someone killing another person over pennies is just hilarious. I can't even imagine her telling that story to her fellow inmates in prison. But yeah, hopefully Jervis is getting some crucial information. He had to take this one. If I stay in here any longer, I'll probably end up shooting every living organism in this godforsaken place.

I stepped outside into the night air. The parking lot was filling up, and the night felt heavier than it should have.

Chapter 10 – Keep Your Hands Out of Your Pockets

"Emerson, is that you, man? What's up, *dog*? It's been a minute." The voice sounded too happy to see me. Who the hell could this have been?

As I turned around, I cursed under my breath. It was fucking Merchant. What a fucking idiot. I hated this damn *joker*. As he came walking up to me, I immediately went on the offensive, thinking he had to be *C.O.K.E.* Shit, everyone else from our past was; it would only make sense.

"*What's good*?" I said as he approached me.

"Ain't nothing, *dog*, ain't nothing, just *coolin'*, man. So how the hell have you been? Waiting on Jervis to come out?"

That was his first giveaway. He already knew Jervis was with me. Clearly, he was sent here to deal with us somehow, but he won't get the chance. I put my hands in my pocket and leaned against the car. The only thing in my pocket lethal enough was a pen, so I guess I had to go *Joe Pesci style*. But let's see what kind of info I can get out of him first.

"Actually, he's visiting a friend. I was just on my way to go get him. So, what's the deal with you? What is Merchant doing with himself these days?"

I could see the disappointment in his eyes when I told him Jervis wasn't around. Second giveaway.

"Aw, man, you know, a little bit of this, a little bit of that. Just maintaining." As he finished his sentence, he dug his hands into his pockets, and I could see him grab something. I wasn't going to wait around to find out what it was. In a flash, I pulled out the pen and jammed it in his eye, took it out, and stuck it in the other eye. As I was going to stab him again, he fell screaming. I proceeded to kick the living shit out of him until he stopped screaming.

Finally, he stopped screaming, and as he lay there, grimacing in pain, I went through his pockets. It was a fucking demo tape. I couldn't help but laugh.

"Sorry, kid. I couldn't take any chances. You should have kept your fucking hands out of your pockets."

I grabbed the tape, examining it as I walked away. Who the fuck uses tapes anymore? I thought, and chucked it behind me, back toward Merchant.

"That fucking *bitch*," I spoke out to myself. To think we would actually play his fucking demo — and a damn tape at that.

I jumped in the *whip* and pulled up to the front. I noticed Jervis coming out.

"Get in, we need to *bounce*!" I yelled out the car window. "I thought Merchant was trying to murder me!"

I didn't even respond to Emerson; I just shook my head.

Chapter 11 – OshKosh and Blood

Driving away from Déjà Vu, Jervis said, "I got some more info. We have to head back to the *Acres*. There's some kid named Pablo we need to talk to." I looked out the window, my mind wandering.

Jervis seemed a little detached. Not surprising — the stress of everything that's happened is wearing on both of us. I highly doubt we'll be getting a good night's sleep anytime soon.

"Did she say who this kid was? Or what his connection to all of this was?" I asked.

"No. She just said he'd have some valuable info and could possibly be an important asset," Jervis replied. "Not really expecting this to pan out, though. I mean, how trustworthy can a stripper be?"

Anyway, we reached the *Acres* in no time. Not many cops out, so the speed limits were optional.

"Okay, Jervis, did she give an address?" I asked as I began driving slowly through.

"1912 Farmer Street. Should be two blocks over. When you get close, kill the lights," Jervis said.

Three houses away, lights killed. I tiptoed the car through the front gate, stopping about twenty feet from the residence. Time to walk it. Emerson got out first; I followed. Lights in the house were on. Five feet away, lights went off. We ducked behind a *busty tree* as the front door swung open.

"Who the fuck is out there?" someone yelled from the doorway.

Turning the lights out wasn't very smart on their part. It was pitch-dark outside. I whispered to Emerson, telling him to move in as I responded, attempting a distraction.

"Look, my car is making funny noises like it wants to die, and I can't get a signal on my cell out here. I just need to use your phone, please," I said. I kept using "I" to make it seem as if I was alone.

He responded very hostilely: "I don't know you! Now get off of my pr—" He stopped mid-sentence, then I heard a loud thump.

Then I heard Emerson: "*Allahu Akbar*!" That was the signal letting me know he'd neutralized the target.

As we bolted through the front door, there were three crackheads sitting on the couch in the living room. Obviously, they were severely under the influence of whichever drug was their poison. By the looks on their faces and the smell of the joint, I figured they were shooting and smoking heroin. Ah, the good ol' *Acres*.

I started to ask where Pablo was but was cut off when a midget walked out of the bedroom with a nasty-looking, naked-ass crackhead behind him.

"Who the fuck are you guys, and what are you doing in *mi casa, essay*!" the little person yelled out.

Immediately realizing that it was Pablo, Jervis went to work. Before I knew it, the crackhead that was walking behind him was laid out, and Pablo had already been tied up and lacerated several times. Jervis always wanted to torture a midget, and for a couple of minutes, amidst all this craziness, he seemed kind of happy.

I know we've been going through a lot today, but this was the greatest stress reliever. Emerson didn't even blink when I started in on this *man-baby*. He was tough, though. It took a while to crack him. I went to the refrigerator to see if there was anything I could utilize. Then I saw them, crawling in a bucket near the fridge: baby crabs. I took the bucket and walked out of the kitchen. The smile on my face grew larger the closer I got to *Strawberry Shortcake*. I set the bucket down in front of him.

"What the fuck are you gonna do with those?" he asked angrily.

I didn't respond. I just walked behind him and pulled down his OshKosh B'gosh pants.

"Hey! I ain't no *fanny bandit*! Stay outta my *black hole*!" he yelled.

I grabbed the bucket, scooped up one of the baby crabs, and slowly inserted it into his anus. I only put it in halfway; I let it walk the rest of the way.

"AHHHHHHHHHHHH SHIT, DUDE!!!! SO NOT COOL!!!! STOOOOOOOOOOOOOOOOOOOOOOOOOOOP! I'LL TELL YA!! I'LL TELL YA!!!!" he screamed as he somehow shitted out everything but the crab.

I grabbed a turkey baster and sucked it out. "Now, unless you want my partner to start round two, I suggest you *spill it*!" I said as Jervis walked to the kitchen to wash his hands. Midget poop. Ew.

"Okay, okay. All I know about *C.O.K.E.* is that the leader is a *bird*," he said.

"What? Don't bullshit me, man!" I said, raising my clenched fist, ready to bop him.

"No, no, really. I don't know her *government name*. Just her code… *Gasol*," he shot back quickly.

I looked over my shoulder at Jervis and said, "We've got to go." He just nodded while walking toward the door.

"You really think it's possible for *Gasol* to run such a sophisticated organization?" I asked Emerson as I sat in the driver's seat.

"How else would that *baby-man* have her code?" he responded. "It's… it's just insane that *Gasol* is the sole leader of *C.O.K.E.*"

Jervis had a look of anger and frustration on his face, but I could see for a second he admired the whole plot as well.

"Well, *partner*, what do you think?" I asked.

"This is a lot deeper than we thought, and if this *bird* is really behind this whole thing, then my guess is we haven't seen anything yet," Jervis answered.

Chapter 12 – Pea Brain

I turned to Jervis. "It's *Gasol*," I said.

Jervis nodded. "Let's head to Providence Lakes in Brandon. I know someone there who could possibly help track down *Gasol*."

Track *Gasol* down, I thought to myself. I can't believe me and Jervis have to track her down. What she and her *goons* have done are the actions of deranged individuals. *C.O.K.E.* is a bunch of dudes running around slapping, shooting, kidnapping, stabbing, sodomizing, and/or jumping anyone engaging in what they would view as nonsense.

For instance, take some *black chick* in a supermarket letting her four-year-old run around unattended while she gossips on the phone and shops for cornbread and black-eyed peas… *C.O.K.E.* sees that. They're everywhere. In fact, one of the store's stockers is a member. And he's watching this *idiot* yap away on aisle 13 while her *embryo* is on aisle 4 knocking cans of biscuits off the damn shelves.

The supermarket/*C.O.K.E.* member walks over to aisle 13 and tips the ignorant woman's cart over, and out spills five cans of black-eyed peas, three boxes of cornbread, four packs of *doo-rags*, and two jars of *black-people hair grease*. She looks stunned.

"OH, YOU DONE FUCKED UP! I'M FROM THE SOUTHSIDE, BITCH! IT'S ON NOW!" she yells as she starts taking out her earrings. "IT'S OVER NOW! IT'S OVER NOW!" she continues.

The member just stands there, looking unimpressed as she hollers and walks toward him. As soon as she gets within arm's length, he reaches out and grabs her by the neck, then slams her to the ground in one swift motion. He reaches over, grabs a box of cornbread, tears it open, and begins sprinkling it all over her body before picking up two cans of peas — one for each hand — and carries out a thrashing the likes of which the most sadistic man on earth would be appalled.

The mixture of brain matter and peas… disgusting. *Pea brain*, ha. But that's *C.O.K.E.* — ruthless. And *Gasol* is their *head honcho*.

So what the fuck do we do now? What the hell is the plan? If *Gasol* and her network is that merciless, then we're in for some *deep shit*. This fucking *bird* is really warped in the head, so predictability is out the window.

"So, what do you think? We should probably go back to the hotel and get changed. We definitely need to check out of there and start covering our tracks as soon as possible. I bet if we call *Big Tiba*, he'll have resources for us to use and undisclosed locations for us to go to. If there's one person in this *podunk town* that *C.O.K.E.* hasn't gotten its clutches on, I'm sure it's him. So, I say that's the plan. What do you think?"

Jervis nodded. He was being unusually quiet, like he normally is when he's formulating a strategy. He had something brewing, and I couldn't wait to hear it — because we damn sure needed something beyond what I just threw out there. We're starting to run out of people to connect with, and our options are dwindling. Or are they?

We've been caught up in a melee of shit over the past few days, and it's been hard to think. But for now, the *Tiba card* should prove to be handy.

Chapter 13 – Six Levels to Hell

I knew Emerson was out of ideas. *Tiba* was our last resort, our *ace in the hole*. He wasn't to be disturbed unless things were completely *FUBAR*. And they weren't. At least, not yet. Our hand wasn't completely gone — we still had some 8s and 3s left.

"Where are we going? This isn't the way to *Tiba's*," I said to Jervis.

I didn't know where he was going, but by him bypassing *Tiba's den*, I knew he had some direction. This started off about us talking down an old acquaintance but had quickly spiraled into something completely else. Vinny wasn't a lone serial killer — he was part of a *pack*. A *pack* of serial killers. Was there ever such a thing? How many were there? How many bodies? We needed clarity. We needed… *Dr. J*.

And that's where we were headed. Jervis was already a step ahead of me. We just looked at each other and nodded — connected thoughts.

Back in the *Acres*, we twisted and turned down *crusty road* after *crusty road*, passing Mexicans wearing Tupac shirts and *dirty birds* with no real body shape wearing *coochie cutters* and flip-flops. Gross. Finally, pulling into the driveway, we saw *Dr. J* sitting on his front porch, drinking a beer and petting the cat on his lap like some diabolical genius. He had on a *Tryphace* T-shirt and a *Ricky Bobby* hat.

"What's up, man?" I said as me and Emerson approached him.

"I heard y'all were back in town. I was wondering when y'all would get around to getting here. But since y'all are, I'm guessing y'all are almost at the end of your rope," he said.

"Me and Jervis need some information. We've been kind of torn *left of center* since this *game* changed. I mean, it started with Vinny. Now there's so many involved… and *Gasol* is the centerpiece! What's going on around here, man?" I asked as me and Jervis sat beside him in a couple of lime-green lawn chairs.

He put down his beer and tickled the cat's ear before placing it on the ground. Settling deeper into his chair, he looked at us both, folded his arms, and stared straight ahead.

"Okay, here it is. You obviously already know you'll have to get to *Gasol*. But you will have to go through a lot of people to get to her," he started. Adjusting himself in his chair, he continued, "To understand *Gasol*, you have to know this wasn't about some bullshit breakup with her boyfriend. It was actually about her little brother, Marco. A year ago, some idiot who was texting and driving ran a red light and killed him instantly. The driver got six months in *juvie*. *Gasol* saw him online a week after he got out, bragging about it.

"That broke something in her. She decided that if the law wouldn't punish the nonsensical idiots destroying the world, she would. Her boyfriend couldn't handle the darkness that grew in her, so he left. That was the last piece of her old life to go. So she started sleeping with his friends. But it wasn't just about getting revenge on him for leaving; it was about recruiting her first six soldiers for her crusade. Every person *C.O.K.E.* targets for their 'nonsense'… in her head, she's targeting the kid that murdered her brother, over and over again."

Me and Jervis could only look at each other. Damn. We really had to find these *freaks* and start picking them off.

"So what do you think? Do you think we should hit up Atiba or what? We got six sick fucks running around out there somewhere that we have to find." I had a little aggravation in my voice. The fact that we had these six *cronies* to find had me feeling like we had to pass levels in a video game — except in this *game,* we could die.

"Look, man," Jervis said, his voice sounding as tired as mine. "If we keep this up, we're going to burn out. Let's head to the *tel*, get some rest, and figure out our next move. We need a solid plan before the *hunt*."

Naturally, Jervis was passed out on the way to the hotel, which gave me some time to think. *Gasol* really orchestrated all of these machinations. She was crazier than even I could imagine, and now we have to track six more killers. *Or do we?*

Halfway to the hotel, I woke up Jervis and asked, "Do we even need to track these cats down? I mean, Vinny's gone and Dot's safe. We *did* it."

Jervis stirred in his seat, rubbing his eyes for a few seconds. When he finally spoke, his voice was low and cold. "Well, after all the public mayhem we've caused, they obviously know who we are. They killed Bliz just for talking to us. This isn't over until the head of *C.O.K.E.* is in the ground. *We* don't get to walk away. And *they* don't get to live."

www.ingramcontent.com/pod-product-compliance
Lightning Source LLC
Chambersburg PA
CBHW081142300726
48982CB00006B/1036

* 9 7 9 8 2 1 8 8 1 2 5 5 3 *